For Tommy, Billy, Emma and Katie – J.D.

First published in 2000 by Macmillan Children's Books
This edition published 2000 by Macmillan Children's Books
a division of Macmillan Publishers Limited
20 New Wharf Road, London N1 9RR
Basingstoke and Oxford
Associated companies throughout the world
www.panmacmillan.com

ISBN: 978-0-333-72001-1

Text copyright © Julia Donaldson 2000
Illustrations copyright © Axel Scheffler 2000
Moral rights asserted

43

A CIP catalogue record for this book is available from the British Library.

Printed in China

Julia Donaldson   Axel Scheffler

Monkey Puzzle

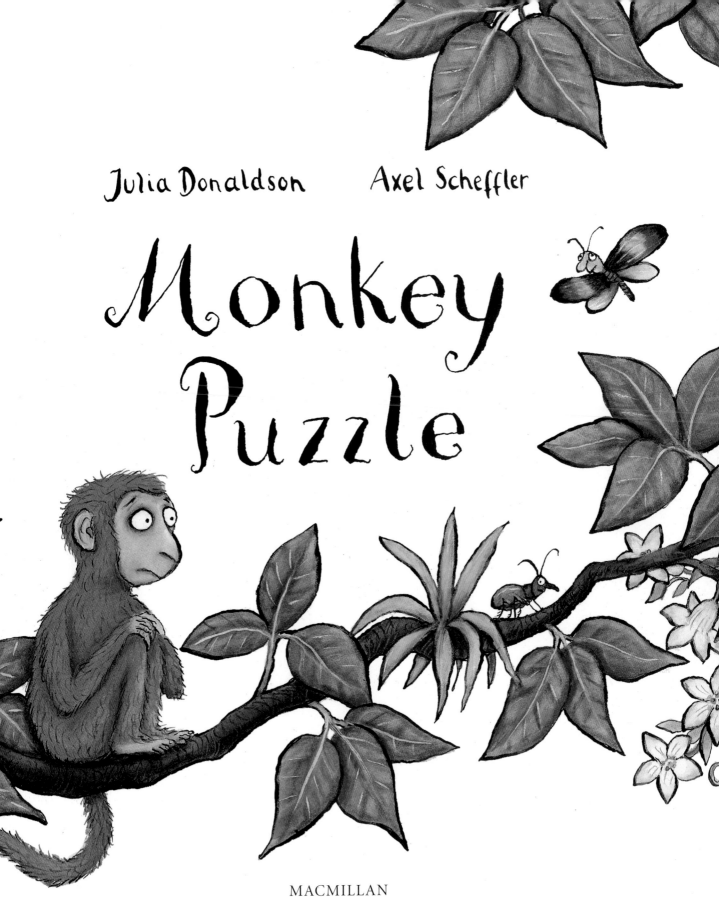

MACMILLAN

CHILDREN'S BOOKS

"I've lost my mum!"

"Hush, little monkey, don't you cry.
I'll help you find her," said Butterfly.
"Let's have a think. How big is she?"

"She's big!" said the monkey. "Bigger than me."

"Bigger than you? Then I've seen your mum.
Come, little monkey, come, come, come."

"No, no, no! That's an elephant.

"My mum isn't a great grey hunk.
She hasn't got tusks or a curly trunk.
She doesn't have great thick baggy knees.
And anyway, *her* tail coils round trees."

"She coils round trees? Then she's very near.
Quick, little monkey! She's over here."

"No, no, no! That's a snake.

"Mum doesn't look a *bit* like this.
She doesn't slither about and hiss.
She doesn't curl round a nest of eggs.
And anyway, my mum's got more legs."

"It's legs we're looking for now, you say?
I know where she is, then. Come this way."

"No, no, no! That's a spider.

"Mum isn't black and hairy and fat.
She's not got so many legs as *that!*
She'd rather eat fruit than swallow a fly,
And she lives in the treetops, way up high."

"She lives in the trees? You should have said!
Your mummy's hiding above your head."

"No, no, no! That's a parrot.

"Mum's got a nose and not a beak.
She doesn't squawk and squabble and shriek.
She doesn't have claws or feathery wings.
And anyway, my mum leaps and springs."

"Aha! I've got it! She leaps about?
She's just round the corner, without a doubt."

"No, no, no! That's a frog!

"Butterfly, butterfly, please don't joke!
Mum's not green and she doesn't croak.
She's not all slimy. Oh dear, what a muddle!
She's brown and furry, and nice to cuddle."

"Brown fur – why didn't you tell me so?
We'll find her in no time – off we go!"

"No, no, no! That's a bat.

"Why do you keep on getting it wrong?
Mum doesn't sleep the whole day long.
I told you, she's got no wings at all,
And anyway, she's not *nearly* so small!"

"Your mum's not little? Now let me think.
She's down by the river, having a drink!"

"NO, NO, NO!
That's the elephant again!

"Butterfly, butterfly, can't you see?
None of these creatures looks like me!"

"You never told me she looked like you!"

"Of course I didn't! I thought you knew!"

"I didn't know. I couldn't! You see . . .

". . . None of my babies looks like me.
So she looks like you! Well, if that's the case
We'll soon discover her hiding place."

"No, no, no! That's my dad!

"Come, little monkey, come, come, come.
It's time I took you home to . . ."

"Mum!"

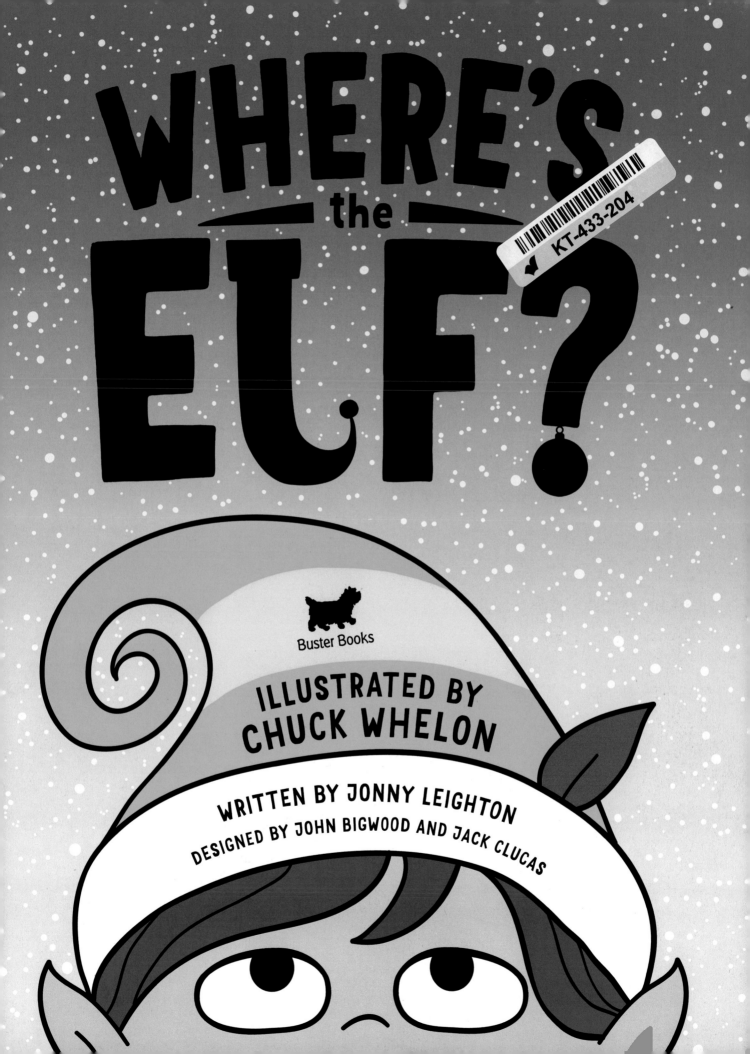

THE NORTH POLE WORKSHOP

Christmas is approaching fast. At Santa's workshop everyone is busy making presents. Soon it will be Christmas Eve, when Santa will load up his sleigh and deliver gifts to children around the world. But Santa's elves have other ideas.

Just days before Christmas, ten elves have disappeared. Without them, the chaotic workshop will never finish making all the presents in time. Can you help Santa find the ten elves hidden in each picture, as well as the bonus items listed in the Spotter's Checklists at the back of the book? If you can, you might just save Christmas.

HE MISSING ELVES

Look closely at the ten elves that have gone missing. Then get the search underway. Santa can also be found in each scene.

Dash
Chief Toy Maker

Buddy
Reindeer Wrangler

Jolly
Chief Stocking Stuffer

Jingle
Christmas Carol Conductor

Max
Chestnut Roaster

Frosty
Snowball Maker

Mop
Santa's Stylist

Charlie
Christmas Cracker Joke Writer

Heidi
Present Wrapper

Holly
Christmas Tree Grower

A Wintry Village

Santa has tracked down the elves to an icy English village. The residents are outside braving the cold and having fun in the snow.

Frosty the elf has started a big snowball fight. Jingle is singing along to Christmas carols. Santa is searching hard.

Can you spot Santa and the ten elves?

On Safari

The elves have snuck away from Santa again and gone on a sunny safari. They've never seen so many noisy and colourful animals.

Santa thought elves were naughty, but that was before he met the cheeky monkeys. It turns out that elephants and rhinos are even stinkier than his reindeer.

Can you find Santa and the ten elves?

On Your Marks ...

... get set. Go, go, go!

The elves have made a pit stop. It's time for some high-octane go-karting and thrilling, four-wheeled fun.

Dash is in her element – she can't wait to get behind the wheel and start whizzing round the track. Santa had better be quick if he wants to catch up with the speedy little racers.

Can you pick out Santa and all ten elves?

Christmas Market Crush

The elves are dashing round a busy German Christmas market. Shoppers are jostling close together, buying last-minute gifts and trying the delicious mulled drinks.

Jolly thinks the market is perfect for stocking fillers and twinkly decorations. Santa wishes the elves would just stay put for a moment.

Can you find Santa and the ten elves?

Surf's Up

The elves are used to snow at Christmas, not sand, but that doesn't stop them from playing on the beach in Australia.

Santa's feeling grumpy – he much prefers the cold. Once he finds Mop, his stylist, he's going to demand a pair of red shorts for the hot weather.

Can you spot Santa and the ten elves?

Snowy Slopes

It's a good job the elves aren't afraid of heights – they're off to a snowy Alpine mountain with steep slopes and perilous drops.

Santa usually travels by reindeer, not skis – he's terrified of falling flat on his face.

There's no time to be cautious though – there are Christmas presents to be made.

Can you spot Santa and the ten elves?

It's A Strike!

The elves are bowled over. They've never been to a bowling alley before, but it's a lot of fun.

It takes two of the elves just to lift one of the heavy balls, but they still manage to get a strike. Santa is clumsy, and ends up throwing a ball into the gutter. He's not supposed to be bowling anyway – he's meant to be looking for his elves.

Can you find Santa and all ten missing elves?

Seeing Santas

What's better than one Santa? Hundreds of Santas, of course!

The elves took a wrong turn at the Equator and have ended up at a Santa convention. They're a bit confused, now there's a sackful of Saint Nicks to hide from. Santa wishes there were this many Santas helping out at the North Pole.

Can you spot the real Santa and the ten missing elves?

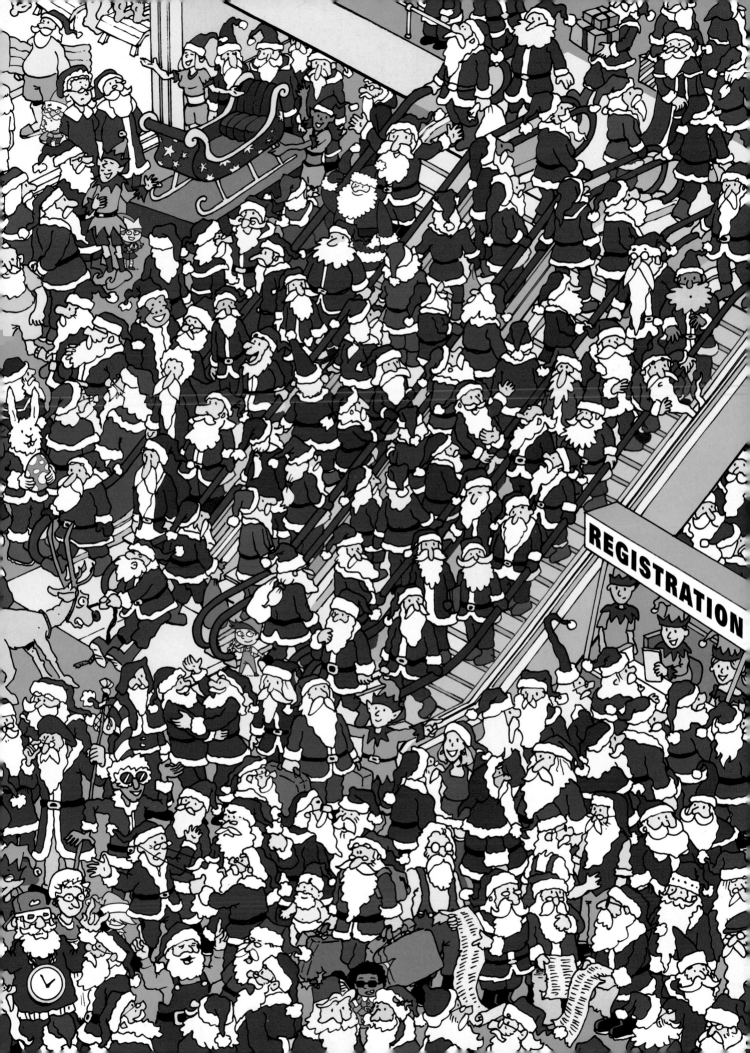

Mall Mischief

The elves have stopped off at a bustling shopping mall. It's full of people hunting for bargains and stocking up on Christmas food.

When Jingle smells all the different things on offer at the Food Court her stomach starts rumbling. Holly is heading to the multiplex to see an action movie. Santa is just trying to keep up.

Can you spot Santa and the ten elves?

Curtains Up

The mischievous elves have snuck into a Christmas ballet. They're amazed by the graceful leaps and jumps on stage. Elves are not known for fancy dance moves.

Santa just hopes the elves will keep quiet during the show – they never stop chatting. He wouldn't want them to get told off by the posh people in the Royal Box.

Can you find Santa and the ten elves?

Christmas Carnival

It's time for a Christmas party. Where better for the elves to go than Brazil, for a colourful street festival?

Heidi and Holly have never seen so many bright lights and shiny decorations. Poor Santa is getting a headache.

Can you find Santa and the ten elves?

At The Museum

Santa has tracked down the elves to a busy museum, full of amazing artefacts. The elves are fascinated by all of the weird and wonderful things that are under one roof.

Buddy wants to take a look at the giant dinosaur fossils. Charlie is keen to see the ancient sculptures. Santa could do with a nice sit down.

Can you spot Santa and the ten missing elves?

Dancing On Ice

Watch out, it's slippy! The elves have descended on the famous ice rink at the Rockefeller Center in New York City.

Dash is a whizz on the ice, and is soon running rings round everyone. Santa would prefer to watch from a distance. He's going to treat himself to a delicious hot dog.

Can you spot Santa and the ten elves?

Up In The Air

The elves have taken to the skies. They're more used to flying reindeer, so they're blown away by all the kites, hot-air balloons, helicopters and even broomsticks, whizzing through the air.

Santa is a pro when it comes to air travel. It shouldn't be too hard for him to track down the elves. Right?

Can you find Santa and the ten missing elves?

Out Of This World

Out in the cosmos there are lots of colourful aliens. Some have googly eyes and long tentacles, others have slimy snouts or twitchy antennae.

It's all getting a bit much for Santa.

Can you find Santa and the ten missing elves?

Farewell Party

Santa finally manages to catch up with the elves – back home in the North Pole.

They weren't running away after all, they were just trying to gather party things to give Santa a big farewell.

Santa wishes they'd told him that before he followed them halfway around the world.

Can you spot sleepy Santa and the partying elves?

France

Australia

Russia

Kenya

USA

England

Germany

Brazil

Family Feast

The elves are stuffed. They've eaten turkey, goose and more roast potatoes than there are reindeer in the North Pole.

Santa's been busy delivering gifts to children all over the world. It makes the hard work finding the elves worthwhile.

Can you spot Santa and the ten elves?

ANSWERS

SPOTTER'S CHECKLIST

Carol singers ☐

Someone falling through the ice ☐

A man dressed as a crocodile ☐

A badger ☐

Someone being hit in the face by a snowball ☐

A WINTRY VILLAGE

ON SAFARI

SPOTTER'S CHECKLIST

A crocodile dentist ☐

A punk zebra ☐

A big cat pretending to be Rudolph ☐

A monkey with a bell ☐

Someone riding an ostrich ☐

SPOTTER'S CHECKLIST

A pit stop ☐

A car on stilts ☐

A man whose hat is flying off ☐

Someone wearing a bat costume ☐

A car with clowns in it ☐

SPOTTER'S CHECKLIST

Someone being electrocuted ☐

A skier in the wrong place ☐

Two people dressed as snowmen ☐

A donkey sitting on a horse ☐

A thief ☐

CHRISTMAS MARKET CRUSH

SURF'S UP

SPOTTER'S CHECKLIST

Two crustaceans pulling a cracker ☐

A jellyfish on someone's head ☐

Someone who's just sat on a echidna ☐

A cricket ball landing on a Christmas pudding ☐

Two sandmen ☐

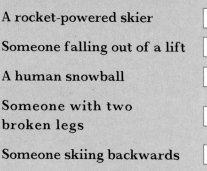

SNOWY
SLOPES

SPOTTER'S CHECKLIST

A rocket-powered skier ☐

Someone falling out of a lift ☐

A human snowball ☐

Someone with two
broken legs ☐

Someone skiing backwards ☐

SPOTTER'S CHECKLIST

A man wearing a crown ☐

A man with a green mohawk ☐

A woman on a dance
machine ☐

A man with a pink beard ☐

Someone bowling
through their legs ☐

IT'S A
STRIKE!

SEEING
SANTAS

SPOTTER'S CHECKLIST

A reindeer who's reluctant
to ride the escalator ☐

A Santa dive-bombing
into the pool ☐

A baby Santa ☐

An Easter-bunny Santa ☐

A Santa with a chimney
on his head ☐

MALL MISCHIEF

CURTAINS UP

CHRISTMAS CARNIVAL

AT THE MUSEUM

SPOTTER'S CHECKLIST

An ancient mummy walking ☐

Two dinosaurs hatching ☐

A dodo ☐

An astronaut ☐

A grizzly bear ☐

SPOTTER'S CHECKLIST

A flying superhero ☐

A film crew ☐

Someone dressed as the Statue of Liberty ☐

An Audrey Hepburn lookalike ☐

Someone wearing a panda hat ☐

DANCING ON ICE

UP IN THE AIR

SPOTTER'S CHECKLIST

A ladybird ☐

A butterfly kite ☐

A cat ☐

Someone taking a photograph ☐

A man hanging on a rope ☐

OUT OF THIS WORLD

SPOTTER'S CHECKLIST

Four sets of alien triplets ☐

An alien eating a sandwich ☐

Three aliens with pets on leads ☐

A lobster ☐

An alien on a turbo skateboard ☐

SPOTTER'S CHECKLIST

An elf playing the accordion ☐

A ballerina elf ☐

An elf in a carnival costume ☐

An elf wearing a scuba mask ☐

A TV presenter elf ☐

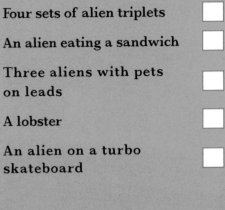

FAREWELL PARTY

FAMILY FEAST

SPOTTER'S CHECKLIST

Someone dressed as a fairy ☐

Someone with an arrow stuck to their forehead ☐

A woman wearing a fake moustache ☐

A cracker being pulled ☐

Someone licking a candy cane ☐

Published in Great Britain in 2018 by Michael O'Mara Books Limited,
9 Lion Yard, Tremadoc Road, London SW4 7NQ

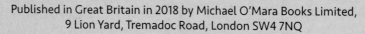 www.mombooks.com/buster   Buster Books   @BusterBooks

Copyright © Michael O'Mara Books Limited 2013, 2014, 2018

This book contains material previously published in
Where's Santa? and *Where's the Penguin?*

A CIP catalogue record for this book is available from the British Library.

ISBN: 978-1-78055-590-4

1 3 5 7 9 10 8 6 4 2

This book was printed in August 2018 by Shenzhen Wing King
Tong Paper Products Co. Ltd., Shenzhen, Guangdong, China.